D0940973

SNAIL & WORM

OF COURSE

by Tina Kügler

Clarion Books
An Imprint of HarperCollinsPublishers

For Lynda Barry

Clarion Books is an imprint of HarperCollins Publishers.

Library of Congress Cataloging-in-Publication Data
Names: Kügler, Tina, author, illustrator.
Title: Snail and Worm, of course / by Tina Kügler.
Description: First edition. | New York : Clarion Books, [2023] | Series: Snail and Worm | Audience: Ages 6–10. | Audience: Grades 2–3. | Summary: Follows best friends Snail and Worm through three more adventures.
Identifiers: LCCN 2022007891 | ISBN 9780358521204 (hardcover)
Subjects: CYAC: Best friends—Fiction. | Friendship—Fiction. | Snails—Fiction. | Worms—Fiction. | LCGFT: Animal fiction. | Picture books.
Classification: LCC PZ7.1.K844 Sp 2023 | DDC [E]—dc23
LC record available at https://lccn.loc.gov/2022007891

The artist used acrylic on pastel paper, collage, and digital media to create the illustrations. No snails or worms were harmed in the making of this book.
Typography by Whitney Leader-Picone
23 24 25 26 27   RTLO   10 9 8 7 6 5 4 3 2 1

First Edition

THE CLOUD FLOWER

Hey, look at this big cloud.

Wow! Look at *that* cloud. It looks like my shell.

It looks just like your shell.
I wish I could keep it forever.

Why can't
you keep it?

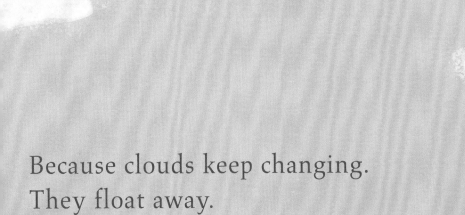

Because clouds keep changing.
They float away.
See?

That is so sad!

Look at this flower.

Wow, that flower
looks just like the
cloud. Let's keep it!

Oh no! What is it doing now?
Come back! COME BACK!

Oh, those are the seeds.
They are floating away too.
They will grow into
more flowers.

But you can't keep the cloud or the flower.
I am sorry. You must be so sad.

I am not sad.
There will be
more clouds.
There will be
more flowers.
And I already have
something better.

What is that?

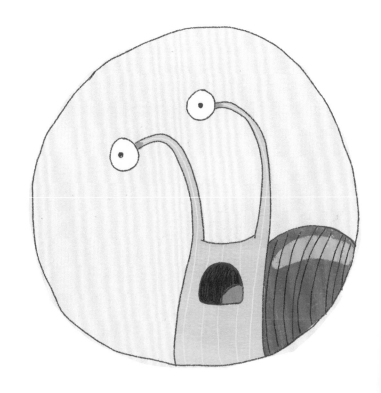

I have you!
You are better than
a cloud or a flower.

Oh! And I will not
float away or turn
into flower seeds.

But if I *did* turn into flower seeds . . .
then there would be *even* more of me!
Wouldn't that be amazing?

THE BIG PRESENT

Guess what?
I have a present for you!

Oh, you did not have
to give me anything.

Look! Look! Here it is.
I hope you like it.

Is it behind the tree?

No, it *is* the tree!
It is so tall.
I picked it out
just for you.

Wow!

Do you love it?
Are you going
to take it home?

Hmm. It is very tall.
And there are a lot of birds in it.

Yes!
Look at all
the birds!
HELLO,
BIRDS!

It was very nice of you to give me a tree,
but I'm not sure what to do with it.
The birds are already using it. And it
really belongs here with the other trees.

Well, you can
look at it.

Yes, that is a good idea.
I think I will keep it right here
and look at it.

TOO SMALL

Hello, where are you?
Do you want to play?

I don't want to play.
I'm hiding in here
where it is safe.

What are you talking about?

It is too scary outside.
The world is so big,
and we are so small.

Oh my goodness,
you are right.
We are very small.
Am I too small
to be your friend?

Of course not!
You will always be my friend.

Whew! I am so glad.
May I hide with you?

Hello. Are you playing
hide-and-seek?

No, we are just hiding.
We are too small.

Am I too big to play with you?
I am not good at hiding.

Of course you can play with us!

You know what?
We are not too small.
We are not too big.
We are just right.